Dear Parent:

Congratulations! Your child is taking the first steps on an exciting journey. The destination? Independent reading!

STEP INTO READING® will help your child get there. The program offers five steps to reading success. Each step includes fun stories and colorful art. There are also Step into Reading Sticker Books, Step into Reading Math Readers, Step into Reading Write-In Readers, Step into Reading Phonics Readers, and Step into Reading Phonics First Steps! Boxed Sets—a complete literacy program with something for every child.

Learning to Read, Step by Step!

Ready to Read Preschool–Kindergarten
• big type and easy words • rhyme and rhythm • picture clues
For children who know the alphabet and are eager to begin reading.

Reading with Help   Preschool–Grade 1
• basic vocabulary • short sentences • simple stories
For children who recognize familiar words and sound out new words with help.

Reading on Your Own Grades 1–3
• engaging characters • easy-to-follow plots • popular topics
For children who are ready to read on their own.

Reading Paragraphs Grades 2–3
• challenging vocabulary • short paragraphs • exciting stories
For newly independent readers who read simple sentences with confidence.

Ready for Chapters Grades 2–4
• chapters • longer paragraphs • full-color art
For children who want to take the plunge into chapter books but still like colorful pictures.

STEP INTO READING® is designed to give every child a successful reading experience. The grade levels are only guides. Children can progress through the steps at their own speed, developing confidence in their reading, no matter what their grade.

Remember, a lifetime love of reading starts with a single step!

www.stepintoreading.com

www.barbie.com

Educators and librarians, for a variety of teaching tools, visit us at www.randomhouse.com/teachers

Library of Congress Cataloging-in-Publication Data
Parker, Jessie.
Barbie : a dress-up day / by Jessie Parker ; illustrated by S.I. International.
    p.   cm. — (Step into reading. A step 1 book)
SUMMARY: When Stacie and Kelly are bored one rainy day, Barbie's trunk and jewelry box lead them to a game of dress-up and a fashion show.
ISBN 0-375-82501-0 (trade) — ISBN 0-375-92501-5 (lib. bdg.)
[1. Clothing and dress—Fiction. 2. Dolls—Fiction. 3. Stories in rhyme.]
I. Title: Barbie, a dress-up day. II. Title: Dress-up day. III. S.I. International (Firm).
IV. Title. V. Series: Step into reading. Step 1 book.
PZ8.3pP169 Bar 2003 [E]—dc21 2002151631

Printed in the United States of America   First Edition   10 9 8 7 6

Barbie

A Dress-Up Day

By Jessie Parker

Illustrated by S.I. International

Random House 🏠 New York

E
PAR

Rain, rain,

go away.

Try on Barbie's
beads and rings,

"Can I pretend
to be a bride?"

Open the trunk.

Look inside.

necklaces and

sparkly things.

A velvet vest.

A golden gown.

Kelly wears

a silver crown!

A purple scarf.

A pretty bow.

It is Kelly and Stacie's
Fashion Show!

Prance and dance

in Barbie's shoes.

Whirl and twirl
in pink tutus.

Barbie claps.

Take a bow.

"Do we have to

clean up now?"

No more rain.

Here comes the sun!

Dressing up was

so much fun!

Rain, rain,
what a day!
Come again
another day!